NERD CAMP

BRIEFS

AMANDA AND THE BATTLE OF THE BRAINIACS

ALSO BY ELISSA BRENT WEISSMAN

Nerd Camp

Nerd Camp 2.0

Nerd Camp Briefs #1:
Nikhil and the Geek Retreat

Standing for Socks

The Short Seller

The Length of a String

Our Story Begins: Your Favorite Authors and
Illustrators Share Fun, Inspiring, and
Occasionally Ridiculous Things They Wrote
and Drew as Kids

NERD CAMP

BRIEFS

AMANDA AND THE BATTLE OF THE BRAINIACS

ELISSA BRENT WEISSMAN

 Olive Street Press

Olive Street Press
Baltimore, MD

Olive Street Press

OLIVE STREET PRESS

Baltimore, Maryland

ISBN 978-1-942218-15-9 (pbk)

ISBN 978-1-942218-16-6 (eBook)

FOR MY BRAINIAC UNCLES,
DAVID, SCOTT, AND ERIC

Dear Miss Amanda Wisznewski,

Thank you for applying to appear on Battle of the Brainiacs, *television's hottest new game show for kids. We are writing with some brain-tastic news: You have been selected to appear on our show! Congratulations!*

As a team, you and two brainy friends of your choice (choose <u>wisely</u>*!) will compete against another team of three Brainiacs. You'll have the chance to win spectacular prizes, and one team will earn the title of Best of the Brainiacs. We will shoot your episode—and it will air on LIVE TV—on February 25th.*

Please see the attached documents for more information about the show, details about filming, and a mandatory waiver to be signed by a parent or guardian.

Congratulations once again! We can't wait to meet you.

May the best Brainiacs win!

Chapter 1

THE MOST EXCITING NEWS IN THE HISTORY OF THE WORLD

Holy cats. Could it be true?

Amanda read the email from *Battle of the Brainiacs* again. It wasn't that she couldn't believe they'd select her to be on the show, because of course they'd select her to be on the show. She was an outstanding candidate who'd be an outstanding competitor and was likely to not only captain a winning team, but to lead that team to the greatest victory ever achieved in all the seasons that the show would air. All of this was evident in her application, so of course they'd select her if they gave her application the attention it deserved. Her disbelief was more at the fact that they *had* given her application the attention it deserved. Adults seldom did things like that correctly, especially in a timely manner, and it had been only seven weeks since she'd applied, and they'd said to allow eight to twelve weeks for a response. This was happening much quicker than she'd planned for—February 25 was just over a month away.

After reading the email for a third time, Amanda pulled up her calendar on the computer. She clicked ahead five weeks and deleted "Follow up on *Battle of the Brainiacs* application." Then she went to February 25 and added "Win *Battle of the Brainiacs* on live TV." She stared at those words for a few seconds, her lips pulling out and upwards into a smile. And even though she was in her cubicle at her dad's law office, and she firmly believed in maintaining a professional demeanor around her colleagues, she decided that this news was big enough to allow for a minor breach in protocol. She rolled her chair backwards and checked to make sure no one was walking by. Then she rolled back to her desk, balled her fists, tapped her feet, and squealed.

"Good news, JP?"

Amanda turned around and sighed. Of course her dad's assistant, Jerome, would catch the one moment she acted like a kid. At least he didn't seem to be holding it against her. He was smiling, and he'd still called her "JP," which was short for

"Junior Partner," which was short for "Very Junior Partner," which was the nickname he'd coined for her at the law firm. It was even on the sign outside her cubicle: "Amanda Wisznewski, Very Junior Partner."

"I heard you squeal," Jerome said. "Is Justin Bieber coming to town?"

"Oh please." Amanda rolled her eyes. "I have *actual* good news. Check it out." She turned her computer screen so Jerome could read the email.

"No way," he said, noticeably impressed. He looked at Amanda and back at the email from *Battle of the Brainiacs*. "Are you going to win?"

"Of course," Amanda replied.

"I knew it. Can I be on your team?"

That was a good question. "I'm not sure," she said honestly. "I've only ever seen kids on the show. The attachments probably have more information about age requirements."

"I'm kidding," Jerome said, patting her shoulder. "I'll be sure to watch you on TV, though. Adding it to my calendar right"—he scrolled and typed on his phone—"now."

The fact that Jerome had been joking about wanting to be on her team was a relief, because Amanda already knew who'd be on her team: her two best friends from camp, Jenny

11

and Gabe. Not only were they smart and take-no-prisoners competitors, but they'd work well together, especially with Amanda as their leader, and having seen every episode of *Battle of the Brainiacs*, Amanda knew that seamless team-work was the key to success. Besides, she and Jenny had both applied to be on the show, and they'd made a deal: If either one was accepted, she'd bring the other as a teammate. This way, they'd doubled their odds of getting to compete. Jenny didn't know it, but Amanda had made the same deal with Gabe, thereby tripling her own chances of making it onto the show. And look, here she was, accepted, with room for two teammates. Her plan was working out as perfectly as she'd known it would, and ahead of schedule.

Jenny and Gabe were going to flip out when she told them. It was just a question of whom to tell first. This was too momentous to just forward the email to them both or to send a group text. No, news this big warranted a phone call and possibly, with Jenny, a simultaneous squeal. Probably best to call Gabe first, in that case. Save the squealing with Jenny for later, when she was at home, or, if she couldn't wait that long, until Jerome was away from his desk.

Just as she was dialing Gabe on her office line, Amanda's cell phone rang. And it was Gabe! Holy kittens. Today was just

12

one of those days. If one more lucky thing happened in the next ten minutes, she'd send Jerome to buy her a lotto ticket.

She put down her office phone and picked up her cell. "Amanda Wisznewski," she said. (That was the way her dad and the other lawyers answered their phones, by stating their own names. Amanda always did the same when she was in the office; she liked how official it sounded. It didn't make very much sense, since people tended to know whom they were calling when they called, but she'd weighed the options and ruled in favor of formality.)

"It's Gabe," Gabe said.

"I know," Amanda replied. "Your name came up on my phone."

"I know," Gabe said. "But *you* always say *your* name."

Amanda and Gabe rarely talked on the phone, but when they did, the conversation always started like this. Amanda usually enjoyed it—it was one of their "things," and they'd probably recount it, fondly, to their children one day—but today she was too excited to linger here. "Guess what," she said.

"*You* guess what," Gabe said.

"I don't have to guess, because I already know the most exciting news in the history of the world."

13

"Whatever it is," Gabe said, "I bet *my* news is more exciting."

Amanda sighed. It was hard to be patient when she was about to give Gabe the news of a lifetime. If Gabe knew what she wanted to tell him, he'd understand. "With all due respect," she said, "my news is more exciting. Guaranteed. Guess what mine is, and you'll see that yours is probably the *second* most exciting news in the history of the world."

Gabe paused a moment. He might have sighed too, but Amanda wasn't sure. Then he said, "We're going to be on *Battle of the Brainiacs.*"

Amanda gasped. How had he guessed? Either her clues were spot-on, or her connection with Gabe was even deeper than she'd thought. They really were meant to be. "How did you know?" she asked.

"Because I got an email from them today, inviting me on the show!"

"Wait," Amanda said, "what?"

"I got an email from *Battle of the Brainiacs,*" Gabe repeated, his voice rising with excitement, "saying my application was accepted. We're going to be on the show!"

Holy calico. It couldn't be.

"*You* got invited on *Battle of the Brainiacs*?" Amanda said. "Today?"

"Yes!" Gabe laughed. "And you can be on my team. That was our deal. I told you my news was better than yours."

"It's not better," Amanda said, her head spinning. Would the producers of *Battle of the Brainiacs* allow them to appear on the show twice, once with Amanda as the team captain and once with Gabe? She'd have to check the accompanying materials, and if it wasn't in there already, ensure it got into the contract. They could add a clause saying her team could return if they won their first competition. Or maybe that they could return if they lost, so it'd be like they were back to try again. Audiences loved scrappy underdogs; they'd eat it up. In that case, she hoped Gabe's episode was first, so that *he'd* captain the losing team and she'd return to lead them to victory.

"What's the date of your show?" she asked him.

"February twenty-fifth," Gabe answered. "It airs live."

"February twenty-fifth," Amanda repeated slowly.

"Got it in my phone!" Jerome called from his desk.

Amanda's heart beat faster. She pulled up her calendar again and went to February 25. Sure enough, there it was, her

only item for that day: "Win *Battle of the Brainiacs* on live TV."
With Gabe on her team. She had mentioned both Gabe and
Jenny in her application, to demonstrate her commitment by
showing that she'd already chosen teammates. Is that why
Gabe got a letter? To be part of her team?

"Amanda?" Gabe said. "Are you there?"

"Yeah, I'm here."

"Are you so excited that you're speechless? I didn't think
that was possible."

"I'm just in shock." Amanda sat back in her chair. "Are you
ready for this?"

"Yeah," Gabe said, but he didn't sound ready. At least
she'd still get to say something that would blow his mind.

"I had the same exact news. I'm also going to be on *Battle
of the Brainiacs* on February twenty-fifth."

"On my team."

"No, on my own team. Are you sure *you're* not going to be
on *my* team? Maybe that's what your letter says."

"My letter says I get to choose two teammates. It says, 'As
a team, you and two brainy friends of your choice (choose
wisely!) will compete'—"

"It's the same letter!" Amanda said. "We got the same
letter, with the same date."

16

"—against another team of three Brainiacs—"

"*My* team!" Amanda said. "*Your* team of Brainiacs will compete against *my* team of Brainiacs." It was finally sinking in.

"Wait a minute," Gabe said, and she could hear that it was sinking in for him too. "That's crazy."

Was it crazy, or was it all part of a grand plan by the *Battle of the Brainiacs* producers? They knew she wanted Gabe on her team, because she'd said so in her application, and they had his application to appear on the show as well. So instead of picking one of them and allowing them to work together, they'd chosen *both* of them and made them competitors. It would make for exciting TV, this rivalry between friends, that's for sure. It was actually a brilliant marketing move; their episode would probably go viral online.

"Crazy indeed," Amanda said. Gabe didn't know that she'd put his name on her application, so there was no reason for him to guess that the producers were pitting them against each other on purpose. Better to let him think it was all a coincidence. It'd give her team just a little bit of an edge going into the game, and she was certainly not going to turn down an edge. Had she wanted to work *with* Gabe to become Best of the Brainiacs? Of course. But that chance was gone. Now only

17

one of them would claim the title, and she was determined to make sure it wasn't him.

"I mean, what are the odds?" Gabe mused.

"The odds that you'll win?" Amanda said innocently. Then she put on her best game face and hoped it translated into her best game *voice*, since Gabe couldn't see her face over the phone. "Very, very low."

Chapter 2

JENNY

"Let me get this straight," Jenny said.

It was after dinner, and Amanda was at home. She'd wanted to call Jenny right after she talked to Gabe, but none of the office conference rooms were available, and she didn't need Jerome to overhear another conversation. So instead, she'd texted Jenny and scheduled a video call for later that night. When they connected, and Amanda saw that Jenny was sitting in bed, wearing her pajamas, Amanda was immediately glad they did it this way. She'd placed Jenny on hold while she changed into her own pajamas and climbed into her own bed. Then it was almost like they were together at the Summer Center for Gifted Enrichment.

"You were planning to have Gabe on our team," Jenny continued, "but now it's going to be us *versus* Gabe."

"Correct."

"Okay," Jenny said, and Amanda could see that her brain was working. "Well, we know who Gabe's two teammates will be."

"Wesley and Nikhil," Amanda agreed. There was no question that Gabe would choose his two bunkmates from camp. She supposed it was possible that he'd choose two friends from home instead, or even his stepbrother, Zack, just to throw Amanda off. But the email had said to choose *wisely*, and they all knew that his bunkmates were the wisest choice. Together, those boys were one perfectly engineered machine, which meant they'd be formidable competition.

"Do you think he's asked them yet?" Jenny said, taking off her glasses and resting her head on her pillow. "I could try to get to Nikhil first. Claim him for our side and leave Gabe scrambling."

That was an interesting idea. Poaching Nikhil would definitely mess with Gabe's head, and his teamwork. But it would also make him and Wesley furious, which would only fuel their fire to win. Besides, Jenny was Amanda's best friend, but Amanda couldn't help but question her motives. Jenny

20

and Nikhil had really bonded at the Summer Center weekend retreat a couple months ago, and if they were together on a team, they might be too busy falling in love to focus on the task at hand. Nikhil was so cautious about everything, too. He'd come prepared, that's for sure, but who knew how he'd perform under pressure, especially with his best friends on the opposite side of the stage. "No," she said finally. "Let's leave them together. Knowing them so well gives us an edge."

"Yeah, good point," Jenny said, though she looked disappointed. "Who should we ask to be our third teammate, then? Vidya?"

Amanda scrunched one side of her face. Vidya was another bunkmate of theirs from camp. She was brainy, but she was also kind of spacy.

"Yeah," Jenny agreed. "She might forget to show up."

"We could ask your brother," Amanda tried. "That would really intimidate the boys." Calvin Chin, better known as C2, was practically worshipped at Summer Center. He'd skipped two grades, so he was already a junior in high school, though he probably could have been in college, he was so smart. But Amanda had a feeling Jenny wouldn't see the advantages.

Sure enough, Jenny rolled her eyes back in her skull and made a gagging noise. "And further inflate his enormous ego?

21

No, thanks."

"Yeah, you're right," Amanda said quickly, to avoid Jenny lumping her in with all the people who idolized her brother. "Are you willing to expand our boundaries beyond camp? If so, I may have the perfect candidate."

Jenny yawned, stretching the rubber bands in her mouth so thin it seemed like they might snap and come flying at the camera. But they didn't, and Jenny looked back at Amanda, one eyebrow raised. "Oh yeah? Who?"

"This girl at my school named Ty. She's new—she just started after winter break—but she seems really smart."

"I don't know," Jenny said, leaning back into her pillow and yawning again. "She's new? It sounds kind risky."

"She is largely an unknown," Amanda granted, "but I have a good feeling about her. I'm confident that the three of us would make a good team." *Please say yes,* Amanda thought. Everything she'd told Jenny was true: Ty did seem super smart, and she would make an excellent third teammate. It was also true that Amanda was eager to make Ty her friend—desperate, almost—but hadn't yet found a way. *Battle of the Brainiacs* was the perfect opportunity. Who would turn down the chance to go on national TV?

But Jenny didn't seem very focused on the teammate

22

approval process. She yawned yet again, then removed her glasses and rubbed her eyes. "Sorry," she said, blinking into the screen. "I was up *so* late doing homework last night, and then I went straight from school to violin, and then I had a *three hour* squash practice. Tournament this weekend."

"Sheesh," Amanda said. "Do you still have homework to do tonight too?"

"Just math. I did the rest at lunch." Jenny squeezed her eyes shut and sighed. "Except for Chinese. I completely forgot about Chinese school tomorrow."

"You'd better go," Amanda said.

"Yeah." Jenny rolled over so that Amanda couldn't see her, though she did hear lots of shuffling and mumbling about where a certain book could be.

"I'll ask Ty tomorrow," Amanda told the bed, "and let you know what she says."

Jenny still wasn't on the screen, but Amanda heard her call, "Who's Ty again?"

"A new girl at my school. I'm going to see if she wants to be our third teammate for *Battle of the Brainiacs*."

"Found it!" Jenny announced. She reappeared and held up a book with Chinese writing on the front. "I'm going to go. But *Battle of the Brainiacs*," she said, pointing at the screen.

"February twenty-fifth. Me and you."

"Me, you, and Ty."

"Right," Jenny said. "Those boys don't stand a chance."

Chapter 3

TY

Amanda's private school was so small, it almost couldn't be called a school. There were only fourteen kids total, ranging from ages six through eleven. It was heaven academically, since the learning was highly personalized, and the teachers gave everyone lots of attention. But this year, Amanda's closest school friend, Penelope, had left to attend the large public middle school, which meant Amanda became the only sixth grader (to the extent that her school had grade levels) and, to an unexpected degree, the loneliest person at school. Without Penelope, Amanda was the oldest and the smartest; the other kids looked to her as though she were another teacher, which was as gratifying as Amanda expected it to be. The problem, however, was that despite her maturity and aptitude for meaningful adult conversation, the teachers still treated her like a kid. As a result, she occupied a strange and lonely middle ground...until Ty moved in a couple weeks ago.

Everyone wanted to be friends with Ty. She was eleven and wore cool sneakers, and even though it was freezing out, she rode to school on the back of her mom's moped, which meant she always walked in with a big, silver helmet tucked under her arm. (Amanda rode her bike to school in the spring and fall, but her own yellow helmet looked like Ty's helmet's baby cousin.) When the teacher had Ty introduce herself the first day, she said she was an "army brat" who'd lived all over the world.

After that introduction, Ty was quiet, but not in a shy way, more of a confident, detached way, like she already had enough friends, but thanks anyway. She participated in class discussions (insightfully, always) and answered the teachers' questions (correctly, always), but otherwise she kept to herself. Last year, Amanda wouldn't have viewed Ty as anything but a threat to her own academic superiority. But with Penelope gone, Amanda was hungry—no, starving—for someone to take her place, and Ty's aloofness only increased her appeal. This *Battle of the Brainiacs* invitation was just what Amanda needed to finally forge their friendship.

So the next day, she got to school ten minutes early. Her plan was to announce her television debut first thing, before the schoolwide morning meeting. Odds were Ty would be instantly impressed, but if not, she'd at least see how impressed everyone else was, and that would pique her interest.

But only the youngest kids were around when Amanda arrived. They were trying to jump rope using faulty technique, and Amanda couldn't let that stand. She got so caught up demonstrating proper jump-roping form that when Ty finally walked in, just one minute before the morning meeting, Amanda was too out of breath to bring up *Battle of the Brainiacs* in any meaningful way.

Her next opportunity wasn't until lunchtime. Most of the kids gathered around the two round tables, but Ty did what she did every day during lunch: sit in the blue bean bag chair, eat a peanut butter sandwich, and read *The Brothers Karamazov*—in Russian.

Amanda walked over and stood by Ty's dangling feet. "Hi," she said.

Ty lifted her eyes from the book, gave a quick nod, and looked back at the book.

"Are you liking that?" Amanda asked, gesturing toward the book with her chin.

Ty lifted her eyes again, and Amanda thought she saw a spark of interest. "Have you read it?"

"No," she admitted. "But I've read an abridged version of *War and Peace*."

"In Russian?" Ty asked.

"In English," Amanda said, well aware of how pathetic it sounded. Why hadn't she thought to read *The Brothers Karamozov* before approaching Ty? Then they could talk about it together, and they'd get so caught up in the discussion that their teacher would ask them to continue the conversation after school, and they would! But *The Brothers Karamozov* looked to be about 900 pages long, and Ty looked to be about 500 pages in, so by the time Amanda caught up, even reading in English, her *Battle of the Brainiacs* episode would have come and gone, and it'd be too late to ask Ty to be on her team.

Amanda could have kicked herself. *Focus, Wisznewski,* she thought. She didn't need *The Brothers Karamozov* to make inroads with Ty; she had *Battle of the Brainiacs*!

"Have you seen *Battle of the Brainaics*?" she said.

Ty sighed and lifted her whole head from the book. "Is

that a movie?"

"No, it's a TV show," Amanda said. Trying to appear casual, like she wasn't even paying full attention to the conversation, she walked over to the red bean bag chair. Then, to give herself something else to do, she dragged it closer to Ty's blue one and sat down. "It's on every Saturday morning. Kids compete in various mental and physical challenges, and they win brain-tastic prizes."

Ty dog-eared the page she was on and closed the book. "Like what?" she asked coolly. "Cash?"

Amanda almost gasped. Ty was business-minded, just like herself. (And not at all like Penelope, who cared more about fairies and nymphs than anything real.) They were going to get along just fine. "Not cold hard cash," Amanda answered. "But they are good prizes. Books, games, educational experiences."

Ty's right eyebrow arched at that last one. "Like what?"

"Last weekend, the winning team got a trip to Colonial Williamsburg, including their own private workshop on churning butter."

Ty considered. Then she nodded. "Cool."

"But it's not really about the prizes as much as it is winning the title, Best of the Brainiacs." Amanda looked Ty straight in

29

the eye. It was time to seal the deal. "At least that's what I want when *I* go on the show."

It worked. Ty put down her book and shifted on her bean bag to face Amanda. "You're going to be on the show?"

"February twenty-fifth," Amanda confirmed. "I'll be team captain, competing against three boys from my summer camp, including one who's my soulmate."

"No way." Now Ty's eyes looked like they were about to pop out of her head. "Your soulmate?"

"Yes," Amanda said, "Gabe and I are meant to be. That's why I need to crush him on this game show. I get to bring two friends to help lead me to victory. One is my best friend from camp, Jenny. But I need one more." She tried to sit up, but it was hard to do anything but lounge in a bean bag chair, so she settled on a sideways lean. "How about you?"

"Seriously?" Ty said. "You don't have anyone else to ask?"

Ouch. Amanda was jarred, like she'd run over a big bump on her bike. Why would someone say something like that?

"No offense," Ty said, which did little good now. "I mean, just, you don't know me at all."

Amanda wanted to say that she was right, that she barely knew Ty and certainly didn't need her; that she had *lots* of people she could ask instead. But the truth was she *did* need

Ty. What if she pretended she didn't want Ty on the team, and Ty called her bluff? Who would she ask to go on the show instead? And how awkward would school be every day from now on? No, it was too risky to play mind games. Hurt or not, Amanda needed to be direct. "I thought you'd make a good teammate," she explained. "And that we could be friends."

Ty's initial reaction was indecipherable—she looked kind of sad, or maybe inconvenienced. But that reaction didn't linger. It was quickly replaced by respect, probably for Amanda's directness.

"Okay," Ty said with a shrug. "I'll do it."

Amanda's heart swelled. "Join my team, or be my friend?"

Ty chuckled and shook her head. "Join your team, for now."

"Yes!" Amanda hissed. "Welcome to the best team in *Battle of the Brainiacs* history."

She held out her hand, and Ty shook it.

Just wait, Amanda thought. Teammates was all Amanda needed them to be for now. Training for the show would keep them busy and give them lots to talk about. Nothing unites people better than a common enemy and, of course, a shared accomplishment. Five weeks from now, she, Jenny, and Ty would be three best friends, graciously accepting the Best of the Brainiacs grand prize.

Chapter 4

WOEFULLY
UNDERPREPARED

"This," Amanda stated, holding up her phone. "This is what we're up against."

Jenny leaned in and squinted. Her face was projected on the conference room screen, which took up an entire wall, so when she leaned in, it was like she was a giant who was bending over to examine a microscopic Amanda and Ty. "What is that?" she asked.

"A phone," Ty replied dryly.

"And what's on the phone?" Amanda said. "A text message. From Gabe. Our enemy."

"What does it say?" Jenny asked.

"*T minus nine days,*" Amanda read. "*You are going down.*"

On the conference room wall, Jenny's enormous eyes rolled. "Yeah, right. Those boys are toast."

"What'd you write back?" Ty asked.

Amanda gave her the phone, and Ty read aloud without expression. "*We have been training like Roman gladiators. Prepare for defeat.*" She handed the phone back to Amanda and shrugged.

Amanda wondered if Ty was relatively new to speaking English. Maybe that's why she was so quiet, and why she failed to comprehend the extent of Amanda's gift for intimidation.

Jenny appreciated it, though. She said, "Good job, A. Way to talk tough."

"Thank you," Amanda replied. She hoped Gabe couldn't tell that her tough talk was just that—talk. She had no idea if her team was ready or not. It had been over three weeks since she'd convinced Ty to join, and this meeting was their first and only practice before the big event. Even if today's practice was productive, Amanda feared they were going to be woefully underprepared.

It wasn't her fault. Amanda had contacted the producers of the show multiple times to find out which topics and challenges were scheduled for her episode, but they never returned her emails or calls, not even when she pretended to be a journalist doing an exclusive feature about the show. Resigned to using only information that was publicly available, she'd found ten full episodes online, watched each of them multiple times, and required her teammates to do the same.

The next steps had been making a list of all the topics and challenges on those episodes, plus the challenges on each new episode that aired, then assigning each teammate specific topics and challenges to master, based on her individual strengths. Amanda had been studying her own topics and games regularly, and checking in with Jenny and Ty about theirs, but neither one was recording her practice hours as Amanda had requested, and it had been hard to get a straight answer about how their preparations were coming. Jenny was always busy with something—Chinese school, violin, squash, science fair, orthodontist appointments—she barely even returned text messages. As for Ty, Amanda's dreams of working together every day during lunch and after school had remained dreams. Ty was as polite but detached as ever, always replying to requests to practice with, "I can't right now. But don't worry, I'm on it."

So today's practice, with Ty in the conference room of Amanda's dad's office and Jenny on video chat at the same time, was nothing short of an administrative miracle. They'd have to make the most of it, because it certainly wasn't going to happen again.

"Let's start with a review of the basics," Amanda said. "Each episode of *Battle of the Brainiacs* has three rounds. The first round tests basic knowledge of various subjects, with categories and clues."

"Like *Jeopardy!* or something?" Ty asked.

"Kind of," Jenny answered. "Have you not seen the show?"

Amanda stared at Ty, trying to stay calm. "Didn't you watch the episodes I sent you?"

"Oh," Ty said, "yeah. I did. I just forgot."

Amanda closed her eyes and forced herself to take some deep breaths. Either Ty was lying and had never seen the show, or she had watched the show but legitimately forgot what she saw. Amanda didn't know which was worse, but she did know neither was good.

"The second round is the physical challenge," Jenny said from the screen. "I hope ours involves a racquet. Like that one where you have to use a tennis racquet to hit balls with words on them into different nets depending on their part of speech?"

Amanda hoped so too. "You'd rock that," she told Jenny.

35

"*Yeah* I would," Jenny agreed.

"What's the third round again?" Ty asked.

"Head-to-head team challenge," Amanda told her. "The three of us will work together to complete a task, both mental and physical. Like we have to spell words with each person adding letters, but the letters are buried in buckets of mud. Gabe's team will be doing the same challenge at the same time, so whichever team finishes first—correctly, of course—wins."

"It's also called the *head-to-head* challenge because it's usually kind of dangerous," Jenny added, "so everyone has to wear these helmets that look like brains."

"Really?" Ty asked.

"Really," Amanda confirmed, tightening her fists at her sides. Ty didn't know anything about the show. Anything.

"The helmets are pretty awesome," Jenny said to Ty, cheerily. "You'll like them."

"Okay," Ty said, nodding. A small smile was playing at her lips, like she was starting to get into the whole idea of the competition, though she was determined to not let anyone know.

"The head-to-head challenge can change everything," Amanda said seriously. "You can be ahead by fifty points, but if you lose Round Three, you lose the game."

"Or you can be *down* by fifty points," Ty said, "and end up being Best of the Brainiacs."

Amanda sighed. Semantics. "I suppose," she said, "but we don't want to be in that position."

"We don't want to be in the other position either," Ty pointed out. "Ahead by fifty but lose in the last round?"

"Well, obviously!" Amanda was getting exasperated. "We want to win the whole thing."

"Yeah!" whooped Jenny from the screen. "And we will! Let's practice!"

That's Jenny for you, Amanda thought. *Optimistic to a fault.* It was her best and her worst personality trait—yes, it was nice to have a voice of boundless confidence cheering them on, but it was that same surety that kept Jenny from preparing as thoroughly as Amanda wished she would.

At least they were going to practice now, and perhaps it would render all of Amanda's concerns moot. Maybe the three of them would be a naturally perfect team, in tip-top shape.

Amanda walked to the doorway and called down the hall. "Jerome, we're ready for you." Back in the room, she looked at the screen and explained, "I asked my assistant to prepare

37

some practice challenges for us."

Jerome arrived in the conference room carrying a large cardboard box overflowing with supplies. There were plates, cups, tennis balls, frisbees, toilet paper, butterfly nets—and that was just the top layer. He'd clearly taken his assignment seriously. Amanda's hopes were higher already.

"All right, Brainiacs," Jerome said, rubbing his hands together. "Are you ready to be challenged?"

"Yeah!" Jenny shouted. She held out her (enormous) fist, and Jerome ran up to the screen and bumped it with his.

"Whoo!" he shouted. "Let's start with Round One: Best at the Brainy Facts." He reached into his back pocket and whipped out a stack of index cards. "We've got three categories to choose from today: Film Noir, 90s Music, and Tort Law."

Three faces—two in the room and one on the screen—stared blankly at Jerome.

"Music from the *1790s*?" Jenny asked hopefully. "Like, Beethoven's early work?"

Ty shifted her blank look from Jerome to Jenny.

"No," Jerome said. "Music from the 1990s. Alternative, grunge, hip hop. You know."

"I *don't* know," Amanda said, deflated. "Do you?" she

asked Ty.

Ty put up her hands. "I was born in 2005."

"Really?" Jerome said. "Not one of you knows anything about 90s music? How about film noir?" He flipped through his note cards and pulled out one that he must have considered easy. "Which 1941 detective movie is largely considered the first film to use the 'noir' style definitively?"

"I have no idea," Jenny said.

"Me neither," said Amanda. "Ty?"

"I was born in 2005," Ty repeated. "Do you have any questions about stuff we actually know about?" she asked Jerome. "Like…U.S. History, or Russian literature?"

"Planets," Jenny added, "or presidents?"

"Estate law is one thing," Amanda said, "but really, Jerome? *Torts?*"

"I didn't have time to do much research," he explained, "so I picked categories *I* know a lot about."

Amanda sighed and sank down into a chair. "I've never seen these categories on *Battle of the Brainiacs*," she said, trying to stay positive. But she silently added, *But there's no reason they couldn't be.* What if she and her teammates didn't know anything about *any* of the topics in the first round of the show? What if Gabe and his bunkmates did? She could see

39

Wesley being an expert on film noir, and it was perfectly conceivable that Nikhil would have memorized some basics about music from every decade. She, on the other hand, hadn't even *considered* these topics in her preparation. She realized, with a growing dread, that there were an infinite number of *other* topics that she hadn't considered either. Geothermal physics, for instance. Or ballet terminology. Energy market deregulation! There were so many more, and how could she even begin to study when she didn't know what she didn't know?

"Amanda's right," Jenny said. "I've watched tons of episodes, and I've never seen any of these categories. I don't think we have to worry."

"Let's move on to Round Two," Ty suggested, checking the time on her phone.

Amanda's nerves inched upward toward panic. Ty was probably trying to hurry this along so she could get out of here. She probably regretted joining the team, and she had to be losing respect for Amanda with each passing moment. If this practice didn't get better, and Amanda and Jenny didn't prove their worth as Brainiacs, she could kiss Ty's friendship goodbye.

"Round Two!" Jerome announced. "Physical challenge." He held up a finger. "I just have to set up a few things."

Everyone sat in silence while he pulled supplies out of the cardboard box and started arranging them around the room. After about fifteen seconds, Ty announced that she was going to the bathroom. Amanda told her where it was, and she left.

"Is she gone?" Jenny whispered from the screen.

"Yeah," Amanda replied.

Jenny looked to her left and right, then leaned into the camera. "Are you sure she's the best teammate? She's never watched the show, and she doesn't know anything about tort law."

Unbelievable. "You don't know anything about tort law either," Amanda hissed. "None of us knew anything about any of those topics."

"True," Jenny said. "But Ty just doesn't seem into it, A. And think of our opponents. They are nothing if not passionate."

"I'm going to get something from the custodial closet," Jerome announced. He walked out of the conference room.

Amanda watched him go and made sure Ty wasn't on her way back in. "Ty's awesome, I promise," she said to Jenny, even though she wasn't sure how true that statement was. She was starting to get tired of Ty's aloofness, the way she was too cool to care about anything. But it was too late to find another teammate, and there were no other options for finding another friend. So it didn't matter if Ty was awesome or not, because when it came to school, having a non-awesome friend was better than having no friends. And if the three of them lost to Gabe, how would Amanda face Ty day after day?

"Jerome's questions were a bad start," Amanda continued. "It'll get better with this next round."

"Maybe," Jenny said, cleaning her glasses on the bottom of her shirt. "But maybe not. Ty just looks bored. And she's never even seen the show."

"I am kind of bored," Ty said from the doorway. "So if you don't want me on your team, I can just go home."

No. Amanda closed her eyes. This was not the way this day was supposed to go. They were supposed to have a spectacular practice, followed by quality time laughing together at all their new inside jokes. Ty was supposed to ask if she could stay for dinner, not if she could go home early.

"We want you on the team," Amanda said firmly. "We really do. Right, Jenny?"

But Jenny wasn't on the screen. All they could see was her empty bedroom with an open door. Jenny must have disappeared into the hall out of embarrassment.

"Doesn't look like your friend cares if I stay," Ty said. She didn't sound angry or sad or even offended. She sounded relieved, like she'd been looking for an excuse to get out of here, and here it finally was.

Her attitude couldn't have been about *Battle of the Brainiacs*—when Amanda first invited her on the show, there was genuine excitement under Ty's stony exterior. That meant Ty's attitude was about Amanda. She just didn't want to be friends.

Jerome returned from the custodial closet carrying a mop and a broom. He held them up and smiled. "Who's ready for a physical challenge?"

Amanda looked at Ty desperately. "Please stay," she pleaded.

Ty looked at Amanda for a few seconds, then at the screen, where Jenny was still missing in action. "See you at school," she said. Then she walked to the conference room table, tucked her leather jacket under one arm, her silver helmet under the other, and left.

Chapter 5

A FORMAL APOLOGY

The next morning, Amanda brought a fruit basket to school for Ty. It was an elaborate affair, with citrus and pineapple and even chocolate-covered strawberries, all wrapped up in plastic with a big bow on the top. She kept it in her cubby underneath her winter coat until lunch time, at which point she placed it next to Ty's favorite blue beanbag chair.

"What's this?" Ty asked when she saw it.

"A fruit basket," Amanda replied. "It's a pretty standard way of thanking someone in the corporate world. Or, in this case, apologizing."

"Um, thank you?" Ty said, peering inside the plastic wrap.

Amanda fought through her disappointment. What had

she expected, a high five? An offer to split the clementine? She'd delivered the gift. Now it was time to be direct. "I'm really sorry about yesterday, and so is Jenny. She recorded a video of herself saying so, if you want to watch it." She pulled out her phone and started to open the video.

"That's okay," Ty said, stopping her. "I don't need to see it."

Amanda put her phone away and intertwined her fingers, making a praying gesture. "Please come back to the team," she begged. "We really didn't mean to be mean. We were just stressed out because it's so close to the twenty-fifth, and our opponents are trying to intimidate us, and Jerome's categories were so unhelpful, and—"

"They really were terrible categories," Ty said.

"I *know*, right?" Amanda said. "He's completely out of touch with our generation."

Ty gave the slightest hint of a smile. "How'd the rest of the practice go?"

"Below average," Amanda admitted. "The tennis balls had numbers of them, and I was supposed to use a mop like a golf club to hit them into different objects depending on math problems."

"Okay…"

"But it was really hard to maneuver around all the big

chairs, and then I tripped on a power cord and we lost the connection to Jenny, and someone from I.T. had to come get the system hooked up again, and by then somebody had spilled coffee in the break room and the janitor needed the mop."

Now Ty was full-on smiling. Amanda couldn't be sure, but she might have even described Ty's eyes as "twinkling."

"It was a complete disaster as far as winning *Battle of the Brainiacs* is concerned," Amanda said, "but it makes for a funny story, I guess."

Then Ty did something Amanda had never seen her do before. She laughed. She *laughed!*

"Does this mean you'll come back to the team?" Amanda asked hopefully. "Even if it means making complete fools of ourselves in front of my future husband, a live studio audience, and all of America?"

"Don't forget about the people who watch online from other countries."

Amanda winced. "Them too."

Ty laughed again. "Okay," she said finally. "I'll be there."

"You will? Thank you!" Amanda could have hugged her, but Ty clearly wasn't the hugging type, and invading her personal space might make her change her mind. She should probably stay away from her for the rest of the week, to avoid doing anything that might jeopardize Ty's fragile commitment. There was no point in aiming for friendship at this point, anyway; the best and only thing she could aim for was a complete, functional team.

Amanda still wanted to drive home her appreciation, though, so she picked up the fruit basket and thrust it into Ty's arms. "Thank you," Amanda said again. She wanted to add a casual reminder that Ty study and practice this week. She also wanted to give her an updated list of topics to review, or at least mention the exercise and nutrition regimen she'd be following over the next few days. But she didn't want to take it too far, so Amanda garnered all her willpower and simply said, "See you next Saturday."

Chapter 6

LIGHTS, CAMERA...

Holy tabby cats. Today was the day.

The show would air live at 10:30 a.m. The contestants had to be there at 7 a.m., so Amanda and her parents had taken a train into Manhattan last night and stayed at a hotel near the TV studio. She'd lain in bed for hours, pulsing with nervous energy and listening to her mother snore, but she must have fallen asleep eventually, because she was startled awake by her phone alarm and found a 4 a.m. text from Jenny saying, *Toooooo excited to sleeeeeeeep!*

The anticipation hit Amanda right then. Jenny and her mom were here, in this very hotel! Ty and her parents were staying with family somewhere in the city, but they'd be at the TV studio shortly. Gabe would be there, and Wesley and Nikhil. They'd all face each other on a real game show, and three of them would be crowned Best of the Brainiacs on live TV.

As Amanda brushed her teeth and combed her blown-out hair in the bathroom mirror, she thought about mornings spent preparing for Color War at camp, the way her competitive spirit shifted into overdrive. Color War was a quaint childhood pastime compared to today's competition. Today, she was ready for battle. She considered using her mom's eyeliner to make black swoops under her eyes (both to absorb the glare of the studio lights and to intimidate her opponents) but decided against it. War paint might not be well-received by the producers.

She knew she'd made the right decision about an hour later, when the studio makeup artist brushed some peach-colored powder onto Amanda's face and pronounced her camera-ready. The morning had passed in a hasty blur—eating an antsy breakfast at the hotel, finding the right building, riding the elevator to the fifty-fifth floor, being led one way while her parents were led another, being offered a bottle of water from everyone she passed—Amanda now knew what it'd be like if she were a movie star, minus the throngs of adoring fans.

49

(Those would come once the show aired.) After makeup, the perky "assistant cast wrangler" who'd been escorting her around the studio smiled at Amanda's powdered face in the mirror and said, "Next stop, wardrobe!"

"Wardrobe" turned out to be a closet with stacks of yellow and blue T-shirts in one corner, hangers of yellow and blue jumpsuits in another, and a wall of brain-shaped helmets on shelves. There was a curtain pulled across the back so the contestants could try on shirts with some semblance of privacy, and Amanda had just put on a medium-size helmet when the curtain opened, revealing a tall boy with an even taller shock of dark hair. Nikhil!

"Amanda!" he said. "Is this shirt too big?"

Amanda nodded. The shirt could have held two Nikhils, maybe three. The sleeves fell below his elbows, and the rest hung from his lanky body like a king-size bedsheet.

"But this one's too small," Nikhil said, holding up a shirt that was meant for toddler, or maybe a doll.

"Isn't there something in between?" Amanda asked.

"This one," said the assistant helping Nikhil. She held up a blue shirt that looked just right, like the third choice in every version of Goldilocks. But Nikhil frowned, looked at himself in the mirror, and rubbed his chin. "I should probably go with this big one, just to be safe."

The assistant looked at him for a second, like she wanted to be say, *In case you double in size before lunch?* But she didn't. She just shrugged and picked up the jumpsuit and helmet Nikhil must have already chosen. Amanda wondered if they were five sizes too big too.

"That's everything, then," Nikhil's wrangler said, and she motioned for Nikhil to follow her to their next stop.

"Are you ready for today?" he asked Amanda as he passed.

"Ready to take you down," she replied coolly, her eyes staring right into his pupils for maximum intimidation.

Nikhil's eyebrows went up. He opened his mouth, then closed it again. Amanda smiled at him, never taking her eyes off his.

"See you soon," he said, finally breaking eye contact to follow his cast wrangler away.

Her own wrangler gave a low whistle. "You play to win, girl."

Amanda now locked eyes with her. "Is there any other way to play?"

Once her yellow shirt, jumpsuit, and helmet were chosen, Amanda was led from wardrobe to the "challenge equipment"

51

area. Her eyes scanned the shelves of golf clubs, tennis rac-quets, laundry baskets, and pogo sticks, wondering which pieces of equipment they'd be using today. The answer was roller skates. Her wrangler waited while Amanda tried on various pairs and skated around the room to test them out. (Thank goodness for her old school-friend Penelope, who'd dragged Amanda to countless "fairytale nights" at the roller rink. She'd felt foolish skating around with fake wings on her back, but she'd feel like a much bigger fool if she didn't know how to skate while on national TV.) They added elbow and knee pads to their growing pile of clothing and supplies and went to a room marked CAST. Nikhil was there already, and it was only a few minutes before Jenny showed up. She jumped through the doorway with a flourish, both hands waving. Amanda bounded over to hug her, but Jenny broke out of the hug and stood at attention. "Captain," she said with a salute.

Amanda straightened and saluted back. Then she said, "At ease," and Jenny threw an arm over Amanda's shoulder.

"I got zero sleep last night," Jenny announced proudly. "I'm running on pure adrenaline and twenty ounces of hot chocolate. I'm going to have to pee, like, every ten minutes. Hi, Nikhil. Are you ready to be crushed today?"

"Hi," Nikhil said. He started to get up from his chair, then

52

almost sat back down, then officially committed to standing. "I'm ninety-percent sure *my* team will be crushing yours," he said, "but I've mentally prepared for the ten percent chance we lose, just to be safe."

Jenny giggled, removed her arm from Amanda's shoulder, and wrapped Nikhil in a side-hug. Amanda didn't know which was worse, Nikhil's attempt at trash talk or the way it endeared him to Jenny. Luckily, she didn't need to contemplate it for long because Gabe arrived just moments later. His blue T-shirt from wardrobe fit perfectly, and his hair was shaggier than usual but stylishly gelled, and his bifocals were secured with a sporty strap around the back of his head. A wave of warmth rushed over Amanda. Gabe was here to compete.

"Hey guys," Gabe said. "This is so exciting!"

"I know," Amanda said, allowing herself an excited raise of her shoulders. "Today's the day I'll be named Best of the Brainiacs."

"She's being Amanda," Nikhil explained to Gabe from his awkward position in Jenny's arms.

"*Yeah* she is," Jenny said, finally removing herself from Nikhil and holding out her hand for a high five, which Amanda gave.

"Wesley's here," Gabe said. "He's trying to find the perfect helmet for his egg-shaped head."

Nikhil giggled. "Where's your third teammate?" he asked the girls.

"*Who's* your third teammate?" Gabe added.

Jenny threw Amanda a nervous glance, but Amanda pretended not to see. It was harder to pretend she didn't feel the nervous twist of her stomach, though, because where *was* Ty? Why wasn't she here yet? What would happen if she didn't show up? Could you compete with only two teammates, or would they select a kid at random from the studio audience to join them? Neither of those scenarios was ideal, but Amanda could handle them. What she couldn't handle would be having to forfeit, or having them cancel the show. This was live TV, so *something* had to air at 10:30, but the network probably had a rerun on standby, just in case.

"Smarty!" Wesley shouted from the doorway. He bounded into the room and jumped on Nikhil's back. Nikhil let out a quiet "oomph" but stayed upright.

"Egghead!" Nikhil grinned and gently lowered Wesley to the ground. "Good thing you shouted my nickname before you jumped, so I was braced for impact."

"I knew you'd be prepared," Wesley said, patting Nikhil

on the back. "I thought you might be wearing the helmet already."

"I considered it," Nikhil explained, "but deemed it unnecessary at this time."

Wesley nodded at Amanda and then at Jenny, greeting them in turn with a formal, "Arch-enemy number one. Arch-enemy number two. Are you prepared for a very public defeat?"

Amanda snorted. "Never."

"Keep dreaming," Jenny added.

"Yeah," said a voice from the doorway. "My team has this on lock."

Amanda gasped. Not only was Ty here—phew! here!—but she was wearing a yellow Brainiacs shirt and talking smack on behalf of their team. That's what she'd said, *my team*, explicitly acknowledging that they were a team and she was part of it. Her hair was long and braided, and her hand was on her hip, and her presence was as cool and sure as ever; she directed the placement of her jumpsuit and helmet with a confidence that suggested she was in charge of her cast wrangler, not the other way around. Amanda could tell that everyone in the room was taken by her. Just like at school, they all wanted, instantly, to be her friend. Amanda felt proud

55

to be the one who not only knew Ty, but was responsible for her presence.

Did this mean the two of them were friends after all? Could Amanda introduce her as such? Better not to push it, she decided. They had a show to win.

"This is Ty," Amanda said, walking over and standing next to her teammate. "She goes to my school. And together"—she motioned for Jenny to join their line—"we're going to take you boys down."

Chapter 7

ACTION

"Ten minutes, everyone," came a voice over the sound system. "We're live in ten minutes."

Before this morning, Amanda hadn't understood why she needed to be at the studio so many hours before showtime, but once Ty had arrived, there hadn't been a single minute to relax, let alone do any of the team-building warmups she'd planned. Amanda just had to hope that the yellow team would be motivated and united by the process of preparing for the show. And it was quite the process.

First, they'd had to sign stacks of paperwork. Amanda requested a few amendments, but the network's legal department wasn't in on Saturdays, so if she didn't sign the contracts as they were written, she couldn't compete. (She wasn't surprised to see her mother's signature on the lines marked "Parent or Guardian"; her father would never agree to such lopsided terms.)

Next, one of the cast wranglers had given them detailed instructions on how the show would work. Most of the information was unnecessary for a devoted fan like Amanda, but some was illuminating, like the rule that if you buzzed in to answer a question, you had to wait until the host said your name before you gave your answer; apparently, that extra millisecond gave the sound operator time to cue your microphone.

Getting microphones was a production in itself. A member of the sound crew clipped a battery pack to the top of Amanda's leggings, then secured it with a Velcro strap. Then the woman fed the wire up the inside of her shirt and attached the small microphone to the neck hole. (Amanda stood still and silent despite the awkwardness of the encounter, but Jenny was so ticklish it took four tries and a series of increasingly impatient sighs from the sound woman to get her miked.) Then each contestant had to say a few words to make sure the microphones were working. Amanda, who'd gone first, had decided to recite the Declaration of Independence, and she only got as far as "We hold these truths," before the sound tech cut her off with a thumbs-up. But Wesley recited digits of Pi, and the tech motioned for him to keep going and going. Either his mic was defective, or the people in the booth wanted to see how many he knew. (Gabe clearly hoped Wesley's performance was intimidating the girls, but Amanda kept her face stony, Jenny rolled her eyes, and Ty looked nothing more than mildly amused. Amanda's faith in her team was growing by the second.)

Then it was time for practice: Practice using the buzzers for Round One, practice putting on their jumpsuits over their clothing without disturbing their microphones, practice running onto the stage at the announcement of their team's color, and, for the captains, practice introducing themselves and their teammates.

"Five minutes, everyone," came the voice on the loudspeaker. "We're live in five."

"Eeeee!" Jenny said, squeezing Amanda's hand. "Listen. They're practicing clapping!"

It was true. While the Brainiacs had been rehearsing their entrances, the studio audience had been filing in and filling masses of chairs. (Well, "masses" wasn't entirely accurate.

59

The studio was much smaller than it looked on TV.) The audience must have been getting their own instructions on how to *watch* a game show, because now, from the behind the large, thin wall where all the contestants were waiting, Amanda could hear sudden bursts of clapping and hollering, followed by abrupt silence.

"They're clapping for us," Amanda said, "because we're going to win."

"Hubris is a tragic flaw," Gabe warned.

"A little confidence never hurt anyone," Ty said coolly.

"Nothing about Amanda's confidence is 'little,'" Wesley replied.

"Thank you," Amanda said proudly. She thrived on this competitive banter. It was giving her the exact boost of adrenaline she needed five minutes before showtime.

"Guys!" Nikhil said. "It's Professor Smartypants!"

Sure enough, the host of the show was approaching from the side. She was as tall and gorgeous as she looked on TV, and a hair stylist was walking with her, making sure each wave of Professor Smartypants's long blond hair fell *just so* against her white lab coat.

"Glasses?" Professor Smartypants said with her proper British accent.

The stylist produced a pair of thick black frames, cleaned them on her shirt, and placed them on the Professor's face. Then she readjusted the hair to fall perfectly around the glasses.

"They're fake!" Jenny whispered scandalously.

Amanda's mouth had dropped open in surprise, but not so much at the glasses being fake as at the fact that she'd heard an audible gasp—from Ty! It seemed like the kind of gasp that would come from a devoted fan whose long-held conception of Professor Smartypants had just been rocked, not from someone who knew nothing about *Battle of the Brainiacs*.

Amanda was gobsmacked. Had Ty been a fan of the show all along? Had she only been pretending to have never seen a single episode?

Maybe Amanda was misreading her reaction. It could be that Ty was merely gasping at the Professor's beauty, or maybe Ty's mom owned a fake-glasses business, and the Professor was wearing a rival brand. But something told Amanda that it wasn't either of those things. That Ty was much more familiar with *Battle of the Brainiacs* than she'd let on. Why would she lie about something like that, though, and what did it mean for today?

61

"Four minutes," said the announcer.

Professor Smartypants smiled at the contestants. "Welcome," she said. "Are you ready for a fun show?"

"Yeah!" they all said except for Wesley, who whooped.

"Right on," said the Professor. "Let me make sure I've got your names correct. For the blue team, we have Wesley Fan, Nikhil Mehta, and captain Gabe Phillips."

The boys all nodded dumbly. They looked so starstruck, Amanda doubted they'd have corrected her even if she'd called them Snakey, Moses, and Mary Lou.

"And for the yellow team," Professor Smartypants said, turning to the girls, "we have Jenny Chin, Ty Alton, and Amanda Wisznewski."

"Captain Amanda Wisznewski," Amanda corrected.

"Captain," the Professor said with a small nod and a closed-lip smile. "Did I pronounce everything else right? Please correct me if not."

"You got it," Amanda said.

"Wonderful," the host said with a dashing smile. Her teeth were so white, Amanda almost couldn't look at them directly. "Brandon," she said to someone invisible, "am I coming in clearly?"

"All clear," said a voice (presumably belonging to

Brandon) over the speakers.

"Wonderful," the Professor said again. "And my cards are at the podium, yes?"

"Yes, Professor."

"Thank you, Brandon."

"Two minutes, everyone."

Professor Smartypants's stylist made one last adjustment to her hair and then hurried away. Jenny grabbed Nikhil's arm and started doing some kind of boxer's shuffle. Ty tapped Amanda's shoulder and motioned for her to move closer, like she had a secret to share. Amanda gulped as she leaned in. What was her enigma of a teammate going to say? That she was actually president of the *Battle of the Brainiacs* fan club? That she was going to leave now, but good luck?

"Which one is your soul mate?" Ty whispered.

Amanda was so relieved, she let out a sound that was half-sigh and half-laugh. "Gabe," she answered, pointing directly at Gabe, who then pointed at himself, confused. "I'm just telling Ty that you and I are meant to be," Amanda explained.

"What's that?" said Professor Smartypants.

"Nothing," Gabe said with a red face.

"Amanda's crazy," Wesley told the host.

"One minute," came the announcer, calm as ever despite

the fact that there were only sixty seconds until this room would be broadcast live into millions of homes all over the country.

"Hold on. Do you all know one another?" asked Professor Smartypants.

"Yeah," said Jenny. "We all go to camp together. Well, except for Ty."

"Marvelous!" said the Professor. "What's the name of the camp?"

"Thirty seconds. Places, please. Cue 'Brianiacs' theme song. Cue audience applause."

"The Summer Center for Gifted Enrichment," Gabe said.

"The Summer Center for Gifted Enrichment," Professor Smartypants repeated. It sounded much fancier in her accent. "And you all attend together?"

"Except for Ty," Jenny said again.

"Right," said the Professor.

"Fifteen seconds, everyone."

"This is quite the rivalry today, then, isn't it? Girls versus boys from the Summer Center for Gifted Enrichment. Who's going to win?"

"We are," said everyone at the same time, except for Nikhil, who said, "We'll see."

"We're live in five…four…three…"

Professor Smartypants flashed her dazzling smile. "We'll see indeed," she said.

The lights went out, then back on. The studio audience erupted into thunderous applause. Professor Smartypants winked at the contestants before disappearing around the wall and onto the stage.

Amanda took a deep breath, let it out slowly, and steeled her nerve. Game on.

Chapter 8

ROUND ONE: BEST AT THE BRAINY FACTS

"Welcome to *Battle of the Brainiacs*! I'm your host, Professor Smartypants, and we've got a brain-tastic competition today. Six clever kids are here, ready to battle head-to-head for the chance to win fabulous prizes and best of all, the title of Best of the Brainiacs. Tell me: Are you ready to meet some smart cookies?"

The audience whooped and cheered, their applause echoing through the whole studio. Behind the wall, Amanda felt like she was a can of soda that had been shaken, the carbon dioxide just waiting to escape. *Channel this energy,* she coached herself, *towards winning.*

"Let's meet…the blue team!"

The boys sprinted around the wall onto the stage, with Gabe in the lead. The girls listened as Professor Smartypants introduced them. Gabe said that he was from Long Island, New York, and liked to read, do brain teasers, and swim.

"And facing off against these intelligent boys today is... the yellow team!"

Cued by raucous applause, they ran around the wall onto the cold, bright stage. Amanda tried to find her parents, but the audience area was so dark compared to the stage, she could hardly make out the shapes of human bodies, let alone determine to whom those bodies belonged. She could, however, see the cameras, which were big and boxy and trained on her, and it hit Amanda that this was actually happening. For real, right now.

"And the captain of the yellow team," said Professor Smartypants, is the extremely smart and talented Amanda Wisznewski. Amanda, please tell us a bit about yourself and your teammates."

Not knowing which camera she was supposed to look at— why hadn't they covered that during orientation?—Amanda settled on meeting the Professor's eyes. "My name is Amanda Wisznewski," she said. "I'm in sixth grade, and I enjoy going to summer camp and singing karaoke." In truth, karaoke wasn't

67

her favorite hobby (it probably didn't even crack the top five), but she knew saying so would make Gabe think of their first summer at camp, when the two of them engaged in an epic karoke showdown. It was meant to be a unifying moment— that night had cemented her idea that the two of them were meant to be—but it was also a warning: She'd been able to sing all the countries of the world, and she'd be able to do just about anything today.

"Excellent," said Professor Smartypants. "And who've you brought with you today?"

"This is Ty, my best friend from school." Amanda asserted it with confidence and then rushed on to the next, less controversial, introduction. "And this is Jenny, my best friend from camp."

"The blue team know each other from summer camp as well. Tell me: Do you all go to the same camp?"

"Yes," Amanda said. "We all go to the Summer Center for Gifted Enrichment."

"So everyone here knows each other?" the Professor said, as though she was discovering this for the first time. Her acting skills were top notch.

"Yes," Gabe said. "We're all friends at camp."

"Looks like we're in for some *friendly* competition, then," said the Professor with a wink at the center camera. "Because only one team can be…"

All together, the audience chanted, "Best of the Brainiacs!"

"And," the Professor continued, "only the Best of the Brainiacs will win our brain-tastic grand prize. Let's see what you're playing for today, shall we?"

Holy Siamese cats. With all the excitement, Amanda had forgotten about the grand prize! She looked above the Professor's head to a screen on the wall. The *Battle of the Brainiacs* logo was replaced by a video of a dusty landscape, with people wearing backpacks and wide-brimmed hats. The people started digging in the dirt, and the Professor's voice narrated: "This week's Best of the Brainiacs will win a three-day trip to South Dakota to go on their very own Dinosaur Dig. With renown paleontologists as your guides, you'll learn about the dinosaurs and woolly mammoths that once roamed the American west, and get the once-in-a-lifetime chance to dig for and discover real vertebrate remains in one of the richest fossil beds of the world!"

The audience cheered dutifully, but the contestants were legitimately pumped. The boys jumped up and down like the floor beneath them had been replaced by a trampoline. Jenny grabbed Amanda's hand and screeched, and Ty laughed buoyantly, caught up in the excitement. Amanda squeezed her teammates' hands and cheered. She could just see the three of them on a Dinosaur Dig. They'd be the best amateur paleontologists the guides would ever encounter. They'd probably unearth the bones of a formerly undiscovered dinosaur, which would then be named Amandajentyosaurus, or something else after them.

"Let's get started with Round One," said the Professor. "Best at the Brainy Facts."

Just as they'd rehearsed, the contestants ran to their respective podiums and held their hands over their buzzers.

"As always, the Brainiacs will answer questions from three categories. Each correct answer is worth ten points, and the team with the most points at the end of this round will receive a prize. Here are the categories for today."

Amanda's mind flashed to Jerome, her dad's assistant, watching the show at home on TV. She prayed none of his practice categories would show up now.

Professor Smartypants announced the first category: "Intergalactic Intelligence!"

Space, Amanda thought. *Yes. Jenny's on it.*

The second category, "Literary Giants," was even better, though it wasn't clear if it referred to famous authors or

70

fictional characters who are actual giants. Either way, they should be fine.

The third category was going to be the most contentious: "Elements, My Dear Watson," in which every answer would be an element on the periodic table. Element Cards had been all the rage at camp last summer, which meant Amanda knew the periodic table top to bottom—and so did the boys. This was going to be a battle all right.

To determine which team picked the first category, Professor Smartypants flipped a large coin that was yellow on one side and blue on the other. Bad luck: Blue won. The boys conferred for a moment, and then Gabe stated that they'd like to pick "Intergalactic Intelligence."

The Professor cleared her throat and read the first question. "With a density lower than that of water, which planet in our solar system could float in a bathtub? If you could find a bathtub large enough, that is."

Amanda had no clue, but she hit her buzzer anyway, figuring she'd guess a planet at random. But someone beat her to it.

"Jenny," said the Professor.

"Saturn," Jenny answered.

"Correct!" said the Professor.

Their team's point tally lit up with a bright "10," and the audience cheered. Jenny beamed and asked for another question about space.

"Once all of a star's material is used up, it collapses on itself in an explosion, creating *what?*"

Amanda buzzed in again, but again, someone beat her to it. This time it was Gabe, and he knew, of course, that it created a black hole.

Ten to ten.

Gabe changed the category to Literary Giants, which turned out to be about authors *and* giants. The first question—answered incorrectly by Wesley and then correctly by Ty—was about the land of giants in *Gulliver's Travels* by Jonathan Swift. The second asked for the author who created the half-giant Hagrid, and Amanda *finally* had a chance to speak. "J. K. Rowling" was probably the easiest answer so far, so it didn't showcase her breadth of knowledge, but it felt good to earn her team some points and confirm that her buzzer was, in fact, operational.

"Category please," Professor Smartypants said to Amanda.

Amanda looked at her teammates, then narrowed her eyes and stared down the boys. Time to make things interesting. "Elements, my dear Watson."

"Elements!" the Professor announced. Then she read the first question. Or started to, at least. "Number two on the periodic table, this—" The Professor stopped and turned, surprised, to the boys, where a buzzer had already sounded. "Nikhil?" she said.

"Helium," he answered.

"Correct!"

"Elements again, please," Nikhil said.

Amanda took a breath and readied her buzzing hand.

"The first of the transition metals—"

Buzz. Nikhil again.

"Scandium," he said.

"Correct."

Oh no, Amanda thought. *What have I done?*

Nikhil got three more like this—buzz, buzz, buzz—so sure in his answers he didn't even wait for the Professor to finish the questions, just to be safe. The score was sixty to thirty, with time for only one more question in this round. Luckily, that category was exhausted, so Nikhil had to choose something else. He picked "Intergalactic Intelligence," and Amanda, desperate to take control of the board, buzzed in before the Professor had a chance to get to the meat of the question. All she had to go on was, "On which planet," which meant the odds were only one in eight that she'd get it right.

"Uranus?" Amanda guessed, trying to sound confident and imagining, in the pause after she spoke, the way the crowd would flip out if that was, in fact, the correct planet.

But it wasn't, and the audience said "Ohh!" and the boys were given the next guess, and they got to hear the entire question first, which was "On which planet is one day longer than one year?" The answer was Venus, because Venus takes longer to rotate once on its axis than to orbit once around the sun. Amanda knew it, and Jenny definitely knew it, and Ty probably knew it too. But none of that mattered because Wesley knew it, and Round One was over, with the girls losing seventy to thirty.

The boys each won a basket of books that weren't yet available in stores or libraries, and the girls had to clap politely and pretend everything was okay even though they hadn't yet won anything and they were behind by forty points and it was all Amanda's fault.

Chapter 9

ROUND TWO: THE PHYSICAL CHALLENGE

Amanda could have spent the entire commercial break apologizing, but there was no time. All six contestants had to put on their helmets, adjust and test their microphones, and swap their sneakers for their roller skates. The cast wranglers helped and hurried them, but they refused to answer questions about what was to come in Round Two. Amanda was fastening a set of knee pads at the "one minute" announcement, tightening her elbow pads at "thirty seconds," and finding her balance as the studio audience clapped a beat.

She tried to gauge her teammates' emotional states as Professor Smartypants welcomed everyone back and recapped the grand prize for viewers just tuning in, but it was hard enough staying upright in her roller skates and trying to figure out the meaning of all the new things around the stage. What on earth did this challenge entail?

"The Blue team is ahead by forty points as we move into Round Two: The Physical Challenge! Here's what we have in *mind* for today."

Let it go, Wisznewski, Amanda told herself. What had happened in Round One didn't matter now. If she focused on the present, they could roll over the competition—literally.

"As you see here in the center of the stage," the Professor began, "we have three bins full of large tiles. This blue bin has blue tiles with numbers on them. This yellow bin is full of yellow tiles with numbers on them. And this center bin is full of tiles with symbols for basic mathematical operations— we've got plus, minus, times, and divided by."

Amanda was laser-focused. She'd never seen this challenge on the show before. It must have been new.

"In each corner of the stage," the Professor continued, "there's a large board with a number on top. *Three,*" she said, pointing to one corner, "*ten, twenty-five,* and *fifty.* In this challenge, you will take numbered tiles from your team's bin— blue from blue, and yellow from yellow. You'll then find a mathematical symbol that you can use to create an equation that will equal one of the numbers on the large boards. For example." She took the two top tiles from the blue bin, which were clearly placed there for this very example, and held them up. "Five and two." She reached into the center bin and pulled out a subtraction sign. Then she walked to the corner with the large board that said "3" and placed the tiles in her hands onto the board in order: "Five minus two equals…" She pointed to the top of the board, and everyone said, "Three."

Okay, Amanda thought. *Piece of cake.* The points would be rolling in.

"When you make an equation that equals three, you will receive three points," the Professor continued. "Equations that equal ten are worth ten points. Equations that equal twenty-five are worth twenty-five points, and equations that equal fifty are worth—you guessed it—fifty points!"

The audience cheered, and Amanda gave her teammates a serious nod. Just one more fifty-point equation than Gabe, and the girls would make up for all of Round One! But the tiles only seemed to have single-digit numbers. It would require a lot of math to make an equation equally fifty. In the time it took to build one fifty-point equation, the boys might make three twenty-five-point equations, or a few ten-pointers.

"You will work as individuals and have five minutes to

77

make as many equations as you can. When time's up, every correct equation in your team's color will earn you points."

Amanda's mind was racing, trying to figure out the best approach. It was probably smart to ignore the three-point board entirely, but what if one three-point equation made the difference between winning and losing this round? Maybe one of them should focus on small point equations and another on bigger ones…. If only they could take a few minutes to strategize as a team.

The Professor pointed to a large clock that read 5:00. "Ready…set…," she said. "Go!"

Music clicked on, the clock changed to "4:59," and all strategy was out the window.

Amanda rolled to the yellow basket and grabbed the first two tiles she saw: 6 and 7. She did some quick calculations.

6+7=13

7-6=1

6×7=42….

That was her best play. She needed an 8. There one was, in the corner of the bin! She grabbed it, gripped all three tiles in her right hand, and used her left to pull herself around to the center bin, the one with the operation signs. She elbowed aside Gabe, who said "Hey!" but resumed digging in another part of the bin. It was easy to find a multiplication sign, but a plus was harder. Finally, she spotted one, tossed on top by Gabe, who must have been looking for something else. The × and the + in her left hand, the 6, 7, and 8 in her left, Amanda rolled to the fifty-point board. There weren't any other equations up there yet—her $6 \times 7 + 8$ was the first. Fifty points for yellow!

Back to the number bin. A 4 and a 1…it was just too obvious to resist. "I need a minus!" she shouted to Jenny, who was by the operations bin.

"Here!" Jenny said, handing one over. "Which board are you going to?"

"Three," Amanda said.

"Can you take this to ten?" Jenny asked. She motioned with her head to a stack of tiles tucked between her arm and her body. Her fingers were gripping the edge of the operation bin so tightly, it would take pliers to peel them off. "I can't roller skate," Jenny explained with a look of panic. "I thought I'd be able to do it under pressure—like those mothers who can lift up a car if their baby is stuck underneath?—but I was wrong. I'll never make it there and back."

"I got you," said Ty, who'd rolled up and stopped, expertly, on the sides of her skates. She slid the tiles from Jenny,

79

motored to the ten-point board, posted 6+4, then skated back to the center, *backwards*, to get Amanda's three-point equation, without even stopping. Amanda and Jenny looked at each other with their mouths open. Ty was a roller skating *professional!*

There were three and a half minutes to go. Time for some professional leadership.

"You stay here and make equations," Amanda said to Jenny. "Aim for twenty-fives and fifties. Ty and I will skate them to the boards."

"Aye aye, Captain," Jenny said. She took one hand off the bin to salute, which caused her legs to slide out from under her. Not to worry; Ty was back. She caught Jenny and stood her upright.

The game continued at a frenzied pace, with the skaters buzzing back and forth like blue and yellow bees around a mathematical hive. Nikhil inched cautiously around the stage, while Wesley whizzed across ("Wheeeee!"), stopping only by crashing into things. Amanda and Gabe collided twice, and their skates got so tangled the second time that it took a full twenty seconds to unknot their legs. (If the clock weren't running, Amanda would have savored those moments; they were straight out of a romantic comedy!) Ty wove in and out of all the mayhem, collecting tiles, delivering them to the boards, and smoothly avoiding every obstacle, no matter how big (the bins), small (stray tiles), or unpredictable (Wesley).

Professor Smartypants announced that there was one minute to go, then thirty seconds, and then the audience began counting down from ten. Amanda booked it to the ten-point board to post her last equation, 1+9. She fumbled with the 9, and it dropped to the floor, and the audience said "Three! Two!," and Amanda admitted defeat, only to see Ty's hands swoop in and—again!—save the day. Ty posted the 9 right as the buzzer sounded, and Amanda threw her arms around her surprising, superstar teammate, not caring one bit if Ty was the hugging type or not. Ty skated, with Amanda wrapped around her waist, to the center of the stage, where Jenny was still gripping the bin with white knuckles.

Only now, with her heart pounding and the clock exhausted, did Amanda finally look at all the boards to gauge how her team did. There were a lot of blue equations—but there were a lot more yellow ones. With her efficient system and Ty's skillful skating, their effort had been flawless. Physical challenge: Mastered.

"What an excellent effort all around," the Professor announced. "The blue team earned a total of 268 points. Go, blue team!"

Amanda clapped politely. No reason to be a poor sport, especially when her team was about to blow that score out of the water.

"But it wasn't enough to beat the yellow team, who racked up a whopping 383 points! The yellow team wins Round Two!"

The girls all threw up their hands, even Jenny, who then promptly fell to the floor.

"For winning the physical challenge, each of the yellow team members will receive a digital compound microscope with up to 1200-times magnification. The microscope connects to a camera for displaying specimens on a computer or projector."

Amanda and Ty joined Jenny on the floor, a joyful heap of cheers and hugs. One of the cameramen ran onto the stage and around the bin to capture their celebration for the viewers at home. After all, this was TV magic.

"After the first two rounds, the blue team is in second place with 341 points. The yellow team is in the lead with 413 points." The Professor looked straight into the camera and adjusted her non-prescription glasses. "But we've got the head-to-head team challenge coming up, and that could change everything. Stay tuned for more *Battle of the Brainiacs*!"

Chapter 10

ROUND THREE: THE HEAD-TO-HEAD CHALLENGE

Feet bare, jumpsuits on, microphones adjusted, and adrenaline spiked, the contestants returned for the final, definitive challenge. This was it. The winner of this round would win the game, the trip, the title, and the glory.

All signs of Round Two were gone. The production assistants had rolled a large wall into the center of the set to divide the yellow area from the blue and ensure neither team could watch the other play. Each team's area had a timeline running along the edge of the stage, beginning at 3000 B.C. and ending at 2017, with eight outlines of boxes in between. Behind that were two inflatable kiddie pools, both filled about two feet high with a white, foamy substance. Amanda couldn't tell exactly what they'd have to do, but one thing was certain: It would be messy.

After a welcome and a recap, the Professor explained. "Buried in each of these pools of whipped cream," she said, "are foam cutouts representing eight great inventions of the past five thousand years. As a team, you must find these creations and arrange them in the order in which they were invented, beginning in 3000 B.C. and ending in the twenty-first century. You will receive twenty-five points for each item that is in its correct place on the timeline. When you think you have all eight inventions in the correct order, press the brain button on your side of the stage. The first team to correctly complete the entire timeline, with all eight inventions in the proper order, will receive a twenty-five-point bonus, making this round worth a total of 225 points for the winning team."

The girls were in the lead by seventy-two points. That meant it was technically possible for them to lose this round but still win the game, as long as they had seven of the eight inventions in the correct order when the boys finished. But Amanda didn't want her team to squeak by. She wanted their victory to be swift and sweet. If only they had goggles to wear with their jumpsuits, she'd dive into that whipped cream pool headfirst.

"On your brainy marks," said the Professor. "Get your brains set. Begin!"

"Let's make a plan of action," Amanda said.

But she was speaking to no one. Her teammates were already wading through whipped cream. "I found something!" Jenny shouted, raising a clump of white foam.

Amanda grabbed the foam invention and wiped it on the front of her jumpsuit until it resembled an object. "It's a lightbulb!" she shouted. She noticed a label on the bottom that said, ELECTRIC LIGHTBULB, confirming her description. "The electric lightbulb. Probably invented in…" she looked at the timeline on the stage. "The middle somewhere."

Ty climbed out of the pool looking like a walking ice cream sundae. She held out a long tube, its sides splotched with patches of cream. "I found a telescope. That came before the lightbulb, I'm pretty sure."

"Smartphone!" Jenny announced, producing a foam one from the pool. "I'll put it way at the end." She stepped over the edge of the pool and slid, in her wet feet, to the last box of the timeline.

Okay, Amada thought. The plan seemed to be not having a plan, just diving in, finding stuff, and guessing where it went. Not ideal, but it was too late to change it. She plunged herself into the pool.

On the other side of the wall, the boys were taking a different approach. Gabe and Wesley dove for inventions, while Nikhil kept his feet dry, just to be safe.

"Abacus!" Gabe said.

"Ancient China," Wesley stated, and Nikhil placed it on the far left of the timeline, near 3000 B.C.

"Glasses," Wesley said. He put them on, making it look like he'd been hit in the face with a pie. "I can't see anything."

Nikhil removed the glasses, quickly but carefully, from Wesley's face and wiped off the whipped cream until he could see the descriptive label. "They're bifocals!" he shouted. "Bifocals were invented by Benjamin Franklin, who lived around the time of the American Revolution, so—"

"1776!" Gabe said. "Place them somewhere in the middle."

On and on, the teams dove, wiped, arranged, and rearranged. Their jumpsuits were soaking, their feet were squishing, and their brains were in overdrive. The abacus and the smartphone were easy, and the telephone came after the telescope and before the toaster, but the stethoscope could go anywhere, and speaking of things that could go anywhere, there was an eighth invention *someplace* in the yellow team's pool that just did not want to be found.

"Stethoscope!" said Amanda. "Between the lightbulb and the toaster?"

"Lightbulb!" said Gabe. "Thomas Edison. 1900?"

"I switched the lightbulb and the stethoscope," said Jenny.

"I licked the whipped cream off the toaster," said Wesley.

"Help me look for the eighth invention!" said Ty.

"Help me double-check the order," said Nikhil.

"Press your button when you're ready!" said the Professor.

Press your button? Amanda thought as she frantically crawled through the pool. Her team still needed to find one last invention. Where could it be? She heard a loud buzzing sound, and her body froze.

"Five out of eight!" the Professor shouted. "Keep working."

Amanda's heart doubled its speed. The boys had five out of eight items correct. They had all eight items! It was only a matter of time—short time—until they landed on the correct order.

"Come on!" said Jenny. "We can do this." She scooped up armfuls of whipped cream and shook them into frothy mounds outside the pool.

The boys hit their buzzer again.

"Six correct, blue team!" said the Professor.

Another buzzer, and Amanda froze in panic.

87

"Six correct," said the Professor. "Keep working, yellow team."

Yellow team? Amanda looked around her team's part of the stage. They were still missing the eighth item, but Ty had buzzed. What was she thinking? She took a step towards Ty to ask, and her foot landed on a block of foam. "I found it!" Amanda announced, gripping the object between her toes and lifting her foot out of the pool. "I found the last invention!"

Ty grabbed it from her and wiped it off. "Bifocals!" she shouted.

"Benjamin Franklin, 1783!" said Jenny.

"Let's switch the stethoscope and the telephone," said Gabe.

"Between the telephone and the lightbulb!" said Ty.

"Or should we switch the lightbulb and the telephone?" said Nikhil.

"Or should it go between the telescope and the abacus?" said Amanda.

"I think we got it!" said Wesley.

"Do you think we got it?" said Jenny.

"Hit the button!" said Gabe.

"I'm hitting the button!" said Ty.

Both teams ran for their buttons. The audience roared.

Two buzzers sounded, right at the same time. The music stopped, and the whole studio fell silent, waiting for Professor Smartypants to speak.

"What a brain-tastic effort on both sides," she said at last. "But only one of these teams has all eight items in the correct order, and that is…the blue team!"

The boys jumped up and down, spraying whipped cream around the stage. Amanda squared her shoulders and crossed her foamy fingers. It was possible that her team had lost this battle but won the war. As long as they had seven out of eight items in the correct boxes, they'd still be the Best of the Brainiacs.

"That brings the blue team's total to 566 points. *However*, the yellow team still has a shot at this, everyone! These wise, worthy girls will receive twenty-five points for each invention they had in the correct space on the timeline, which is as follows." The Professor walked across the messy stage to the girls' row of inventions. She stood by the abacus and took a step to the left with each sentence. "The abacus was invented first, around 3000 B.C. Followed by the telescope, circa 1609. Bifocals, 1783. *Stethoscope*, 1819. *Telephone*, 1876."

Amanda's heart sank. Her eyes welled. They'd had those two mixed up. She barely heard the Professor finish.

89

"Lightbulb, 1906. Electric toaster, 1909. And smartphone last, with the very first one appearing in 1992, and the first with a touchscreen in 2007."

Jenny placed a creamy arm around Amanda's shoulder. Ty took Amanda's hand in her own. Amanda gulped back her tears.

"The yellow team had six out of eight inventions in the correct place, earning them 175 points. That brings their total to 538. A brain-tacular effort, for sure, but not enough to eclipse the boys. Which means the winner of the dinosaur dig and this week's Best of the Brainiacs are—by only three points—the BLUE TEAM! Gabe Phillips, Wesley Fan, and Nikhil Mehta!"

Chapter 11

THE TRUTH ABOUT TY

Forty-five minutes later, Amanda was clean, dry, and wearing whipped-cream-free clothes. She was sitting in the "cast" area of the studio, and it felt like midnight, even though it wasn't yet noon. Apart from a folded *Battle of the Brainiacs* T-shirt, a few photos with Professor Smartypants, and a digital compound microscope with 1200x magnification, Amanda had nothing to show for her morning on live television.

"We were robbed, A," said Jenny, who was drying her hair with a towel. "Three points. They buried our inventions deeper than the boys' because they knew we were tougher competitors. If we'd have found those bifocals quicker, we'd have won for sure."

"Yeah, right," said Wesley, who was looking through his box of not-yet-released books. "Hubris was your tragic flaw, just as Gabe predicted."

Maybe, Amanda admitted to herself. "If I hadn't buzzed in too early on that last question in Round One…"

"You didn't stand a chance in Round One," said Gabe, who still had some whipped cream behind his ear. "Nikhil knew every single element, my dear Watson."

"I took chemistry at Summer Center," Nikhil explained, "and brushed up before the show, just to be safe."

Ty entered, freshly showered and dressed, and wearing the biggest smile Amanda had ever seen. "Whatever," she said. "We creamed you boys in Round Two."

"We all got *creamed* in Round Three," said Wesley. "Get it?"

Ty rolled her eyes, but her grin stayed put. "We all got it," she said.

"You're an awesome skater," Gabe said to her. "How'd you get so good?"

"It was really popular where I lived in Tennessee," Ty replied. "I went almost every day after school. And when I lived in London, we did this giant skate-through-the city thing a couple times."

"You've lived in Tennessee and London?" asked Jenny.

"Briefly," Ty said. "Lots of other places too."

"That's so cool," said Wesley. "I've only ever lived in one place."

"You live at camp in the summer," Nikhil pointed out.

Wesley pointed at him. "Correct. No wonder you're Best of the Brainiacs."

Gabe came up to Amanda and held out his hand. "It was really close. Thanks for a good game."

Amanda shook his hand begrudgingly. Three stinking points. "Congratulations," she muttered.

Some cast wranglers came in and started escorting the contestants out to meet their parents. Amanda hung back, her legs moving slowly. She'd come to terms with the loss eventually, but there was something she needed to understand now. She waited until almost everyone was out of the room, then called, "Hey, Ty."

Ty turned in the doorway. "Yeah?"

"You've seen the show before today, haven't you?"

"Yeah," Ty admitted, her smile still plastered to her face. "I used to watch it online from Europe. I'm actually a really big fan."

"I knew it," Amanda said, shaking her head. "So why were you so weird about practicing?"

Ty sighed. "I don't know. I'm sorry. It's just…" She put down her microscope box and stuck her hands in her pockets.

Amanda prepared for the worst. It seemed likely that Ty was secretly suffering from a life-threatening disease, and she hadn't wanted to get Amanda's hopes up because she didn't know if she'd live to reach this day.

But what Ty said was, "My family moves so much, you know? We never stay anywhere longer than a few months. When I was little, I'd make all these friends in my new school, and then, just as I was feeling really happy and settled, we'd have to move again. So a couple years ago, I decided to stop making friends in new places. It just makes things easier."

Amanda nodded slowly, all of the pieces clicking into place. It was a lot more likely than any of her other theories, and even though it wasn't a life-threatening illness (thank goodness), it was still kind of sad. "So you were purposely trying to make sure we didn't become friends?" she asked.

"Really hard," Ty said. "But you didn't make it easy, girl. You're the most determined person I've ever met."

Amanda felt a surge of pride. "I brought you a fruit basket."

"Yes, you did," Ty said with a laugh. "And you invited me to appear on my favorite TV show!"

"Which we lost."

"Who cares?" Ty said. "I had so much fun! I won a microscope and met Professor Smartypants. And your friends were really good competitors. You're right about Gabe. You two are totally meant to be."

"I told you," Amanda said happily. "Hey, in Round Three, why'd you hit the buzzer before we found all eight inventions?"

Ty gave a sly smile and shrugged one shoulder. "Just to mess with the boys' heads. Make them think we were closer than we were."

It hadn't worked, but that didn't mean it wasn't brilliant. It was something Amanda would have done herself, if she'd thought of it. She wrapped her arms around Ty and said, "Let's be best friends."

Ty chuckled. "Okay," she said, patting Amanda's back before pulling out of the hug. "But I'll probably have to move in a few months."

Now it was Amanda's turn to say, "Who cares? I don't live near Jenny or Gabe, or anyone else from camp, and look at how close we are anyway."

Holy mother-of-all-cats. She had an idea. "Ty. You should come to Summer Center! Then we can live in the same place for two months every year, no matter where your family moves!"

95

Ty's eyes twinkled, and she nodded slowly, and she didn't even try to hide her excitement. "I'll have to ask my parents."

"They'll say yes," Amanda assured her. "I can be very convincing."

Jenny poked her head back in the room. "Come on," she said. "We're all going to go out for lunch!"

Amanda and Ty picked up their microscopes and yellow shirts and headed out into the hallway to join their families and friends. Who cared about a measly three points? Come Monday, Amanda and Ty would still walk into school like celebrities. They'd show everyone their photos of Professor Smartypants, and they'd talk knowingly about cast wranglers and microphones, and come lunchtime, they'd sit on side-by-side beanbag chairs and plan for their summer together at camp.

Remember, Wisznewski, Amanda said to herself. *Not everything goes according to plan.*

Some things go even better.

Geek out s'more with

About the Author

Elissa Brent Weissman, a proud nerd, is the author of many award-winning books about smart kids, including the Nerd Camp series, *The Short Seller*, and *The Length of a String*. She is also the editor of *Our Story Begins: Your Favorite Authors and Illustrators Share Fun, Inspiring, and Occasionally Ridiculous Things They Wrote and Drew as Kids*. She lives in Baltimore with her nerdy husband and their two supercool nerds in training. Learn more at ebweissman.com.

71690521R00060

Made in the USA
San Bernardino, CA
17 March 2018